Bodgit and Fixit's Furry

Bodgit

Age – 5
Wants to be
  A Clown
Likes
  Snakes and ladders
  Colouring in
  Bear hugs
  Chocolate ice cream
Dislikes
  Cold ears
  Rainy days
Favourite thing
  Blanket

Fixit

  Chess
  Inventing gadgets
  Science
  Carrots
Dislikes
  Sprouts
  Crumbs in bed
Favourite thing
  Toolbox

Story time starts here...

Ready

Steady

GO

☆☆☆☆☆

Goodreads.com

ISBN 9781697609394
Copyright No. DEP635778720516131618
A big thank-you for all the support from family and friends

This is the story of Bodgit bear and his very best friend Fixit the rabbit. They have been best friends since they were very little and have grown up together in Rumble Tum town where they live. Bodgit is quite mischievous and always seems to get himself into all kinds of trouble, but Fixit is usually not far away to help him out.

Today Bodgit and Fixit are on holiday. They have a lot of spare time to go on some amazing adventures together. They have had a lazy morning so needed to find something more exciting to do for the rest of the day.

Fixit had an idea, "Why don't we build a rocket so we can fly into outer space?" Bodgit thought this was a great idea, "That would be amazing !

I've just got to make sure I'm back for tea. We're having my favourite chicken nuggets and little yellow chips." They both got thinking about what they could use to make a rocket?

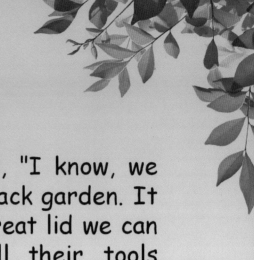

Fixit thought very hard and said, "I know, we could use the old dustbin in our back garden. It is round like a rocket and has a great lid we can use for the top." They got all their tools together in their toolbox and set off for the back garden.

When they got to the bin they found it surrounded with overgrown grass and weeds. They were sure that no space adventurers would have a rocket like this so got to work straight away.

Bodgit cut the grass and cleared the weeds while Fixit cut a door and window in the side of the dustbin and fixed the lid securely on top.

Next Bodgit made some rocket fins for the outside from an old sheet of metal. Fixit got some building blocks and made a control panel for the inside, making sure it had lots of buttons to press and levers to pull.

Fixit finished off the inside and then went outside to see how Bodgit was getting on. Oh no! Bodgit bear had made a bodge of the rocket fins, he'd fitted them upside down!

Fixit chuckled at how funny the rocket looked and then helped Bodgit put them on the right way.

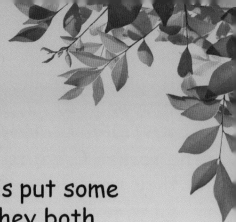

"All we need to do now, " Fixit said," is put some paint on it and we are ready to go." They both picked their favourite colour, red, to use. Bodgit painted the rocket fins and lid. Fixit painted the body.

The rocket was finished and ready for take-off. Bodgit said, "We'd better pack some toys and a snack for our journey." So they each got their favourite teddy, a toy car, a peanut butter white wrapper, some cheesy puffer crisps and a purple fruit drink.

They then loaded the rocket and got in ready for take-off.

Fixit pressed some buttons to start the countdown. 10, 9, 8, 7, 6, 5, 4, 3, 2, 1, **BLASTOFF ! WHOOOOOOOOOSH !** The rocket fired its engines and they were on their way.

Soon the rocket was travelling very fast and the ground below got smaller and smaller until they were in space. Bodgit said "Let's go to the moon it won't take us long at this speed."

Fixit pulled the levers to steer the rocket towards the moon and before they knew it they were there. Fixit then used his control panel to gently land onto the moon's surface.

You are here

Mercury

Venus

Earth

Mars

Saturn

Jupiter

Uranus

Neptune

Pluto

Bodgit said "Let's have a snack and then go exploring." They ate their snack and drank their drink and were ready to go.

10

They climbed out onto the moon's surface where they found that they floated around. This is because there was less gravity than on Earth. They had fun doing big jumps and somersaults. They then played hide and seek taking it in turns to count while the other hide behind large moon rocks and in craters.

Time had gone by quickly, but they had only just realised because they were both having so much fun. By looking back down to earth so far away they could see the light starting to fade over where they lived. It was time to head home. They packed up all their things and got back into the rocket.

  Fixit fired the rocket engines and steered them through the stars once more until he had landed safely in the back garden.

Bodgit and Fixit climbed out of the rocket and unloaded their toys. They had both worked up a good appetite and were back just in time for their tea.

Once they had finished eating they played action figures until it was time for bed. They were sad that the day was over but they still had plenty of holiday left for some more amazing adventures.

12

Mission #1
How many planets like this  can you find in this book?

Mission #2
Bodgit is very forgetful can you help him find all of his words?

WORD SEARCH

R	A	B	B	I	T	F	H	J	C	S	R
E	O	S	L	Q	Y	N	C	H	I	P	S
B	E	C	Q	H	U	J	L	Y	N	A	H
O	L	R	K	S	U	M	Z	W	G	X	P
D	Z	A	O	E	I	M	O	O	N	V	L
G	L	T	N	J	T	D	U	A	W	X	A
I	V	F	B	K	T	S	P	X	R	O	N
T	J	E	P	N	E	S	T	A	R	B	E
A	A	H	U	F	D	T	K	W	A	L	T
R	G	O	S	N	F	I	X	I	T	O	K
E	C	U	Q	S	F	W	M	R	L	O	G
X	C	S	P	A	C	E	V	Y	F	T	X

WORDS TO FIND:
BODGIT
FIXIT
MOON
ROCKET
CHIPS
STAR
SPACE
PLANET
COUNTDOWN
SUN
BEAR
RABBIT
BLANKET
TOOLBOX

Mission #3
Before Fixit can start building the rocket can you help him find his toolbox?

Did you know ? The moon is 4.5 billion years old

Mission #4
Try colouring in Fixit and his toolbox.

46.
47 48 49 50
45 .51
44 52
43
42
41
40.

Mission #5
Connect the dots and see what you find.

.53
.30 .29
.28 .27
35. .26
34 22 23 24 25
31 21
33 20
36. 32 19
1. .18
37. 38 11 .17
39. 10 12 .16
2 .9 13 14 .15
.8
.7
3. .6
4. .5

Did you know ?
The moon travels at 2,288 miles per hour

14

Can you spot the 10 differences

Mission #7
Draw and colour in your own picture of Bodgit and Fixit.

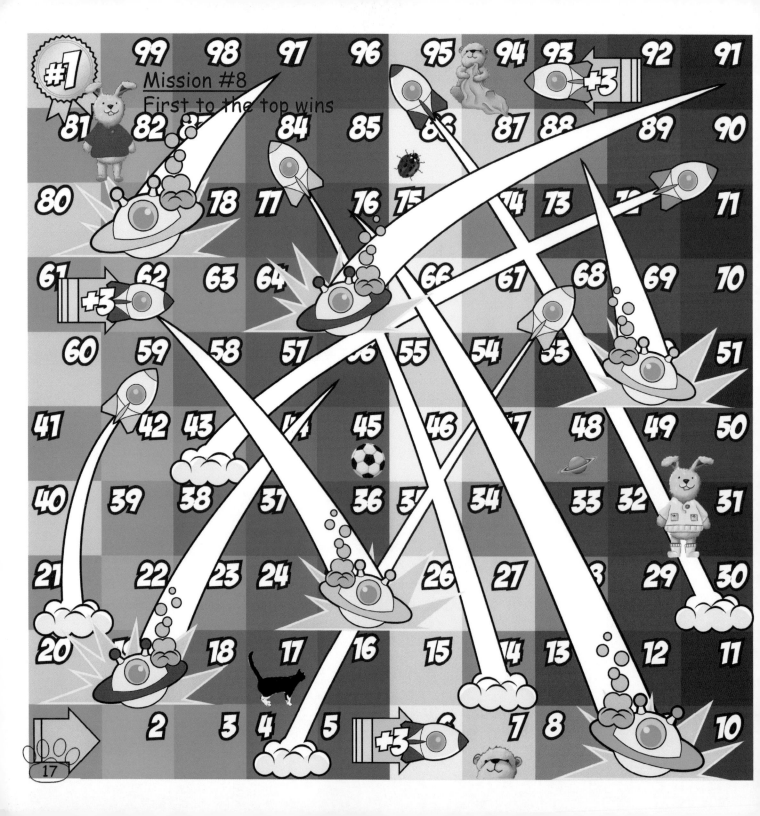

ANDROMEDA

TRIANGULUM

LACERTA

CASSIOPEIA

PERSEUS

CYGNUS

CEPHEUS

CAMELOPARDALIS

AURIGA

LYRA

URSA
MINOR

HERCULES

DRACO

LYNX

BOOTES

URSA
MAJOR

Mission #9
Next time you lookup at the
night sky see if you can spot
any of these star constellations.

CANES
VENATICI

Don't forget to
tick them off !

Bodgit and Fixit's 7 Wonders of the World

Taj Mahal

Ancient City of Petra

Great Wall of China

Machu Picchu

The Colosseum

The Pyramid of Giza

Chichen Itza

Which one would you like to visit ?

Mission #11
Can you work out where the jigsaw pieces go ?

Did you know? The moon is **252,088** miles from earth

Printed in Poland
by Amazon Fulfillment
Poland Sp. z o.o., Wrocław

11168319R00016